HarperCollins®, ✸®, and HarperFestival®
are trademarks of HarperCollins Publishers Inc.
The Tall Book of Mother Goose
Illustrations copyright © 2006 by Aleksey & Olga Ivanov
All new material copyright © 2006 by HarperCollins Publishers Inc.
Manufactured in China. All rights reserved.
For information address HarperCollins Children's Books, a division of HarperCollins Publishers,
195 Broadway, New York, NY 10007.
Library of Congress catalog card number: 2003111851
www.harperchildrens.com
Book design by Joe Merkel

17 18 19 SCP 20 19 18 17 16 15 14 13
❖
First HarperFestival edition, 2006

# The Tall Book of Mother Goose

ILLUSTRATED BY ALEKSEY & OLGA IVANOV

 HarperFestival®

*A Division of* HarperCollins*Publishers*

# Table of Contents

# GIRLS AND BOYS

Girls and boys, come out to play,
The moon doth shine as bright as day,
Leave your supper and leave your sleep,
And come with your playfellows
into the street.

8

Come with a whoop
or come with a call,
Come with goodwill or not at all.
Up the ladder and down the wall,
A halfpenny roll will serve us all.
You find milk and I'll find flour,
And we'll have a pudding
in half an hour!

9

# THE CAT
## AND THE FIDDLE

Hey diddle diddle,
The cat and the fiddle,
The cow jumped over the moon.
The little dog laughed to see such sport,
And the dish ran away with the spoon.

# LITTLE JACK HORNER

Little Jack Horner
Sat in a corner,
Eating his Christmas pie.
He stuck in his thumb
And pulled out a plum,
And said, "What a good boy am I!"

Humpty Dumpty sat on a wall.
    Humpty Dumpty had a great fall.
All the king's horses
            and all the king's men
Couldn't put Humpty Dumpty
                together again.

# I Saw a Ship A-Sailing

I saw a ship a-sailing,
A-sailing on the sea.
And, oh, but it was laden
With pretty things for thee.

There were comfits in the cabin,
And apples in the hold;
The sails were made of silk
And the masts were made of gold.

The four-and-twenty sailors
That stood between the decks
Were four-and-twenty white mice
With chains about their necks.

The captain was a duck
With a packet on his back,
And when the ship began to move,
The captain said, "Quack! Quack!"

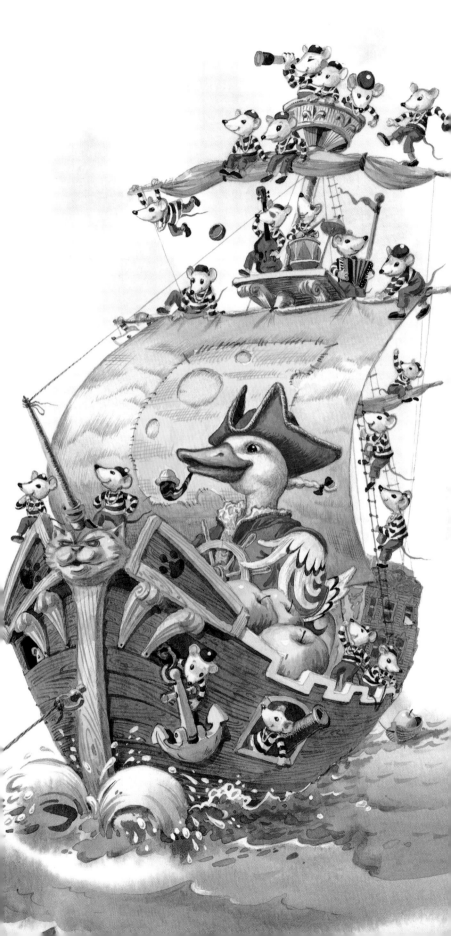

# WHAT ARE LITTLE BOYS MADE OF?

What are little boys made of?
    What are little boys made of?
Snips and snails,
        and puppy dog tails,
That's what little boys are made of.

What are little girls made of?
　　　What are little girls made of?
Sugar and spice,
　　　and everything nice,
That's what little girls are made of.

# JACK & JILL

Jack and Jill went up the hill
    To fetch a pail of water.
Jack fell down and broke his crown,
    And Jill came tumbling after.

Then up Jack got and home did trot
    As fast as he could caper.
He went to bed and plastered his head
    With vinegar and brown paper.

# SING A SONG
# OF SIXPENCE

Sing a song of sixpence,
A pocket full of rye;
Four-and-twenty blackbirds
Baked in a pie!

When the pie was opened
The birds began to sing.
Now, wasn't that a dainty dish
To set before the King?

The King was in his counting house,
Counting out his money.
The Queen was in the parlor,
Eating bread and honey.

The maid was in the garden,
Hanging out the clothes,
When down came a black bird
And pecked off her nose!

# MARY, MARY, QUITE CONTRARY

Mary, Mary, quite contrary,
    How does your garden grow?
With silver bells and cockleshells,
    And pretty maids all in a row.

# COFFEE
## &
## TEA

Molly, my sister, and I fell out,
And what do you think
it was all about?
She loved coffee and I loved tea,
And that was the reason
we couldn't agree.

## CURLY-LOCKS

Curly-locks, Curly-locks,
Will you be mine?
You shall not wash dishes,
Nor feed the swine;
But sit on a cushion
And sew a fine seam,
And sup upon strawberries,
Sugar, and cream!

# The Ten O'Clock Scholar

A diller,
a dollar,
a ten o'clock scholar!
What makes you come so soon?
You used to come at ten o'clock,
Now you come at noon.

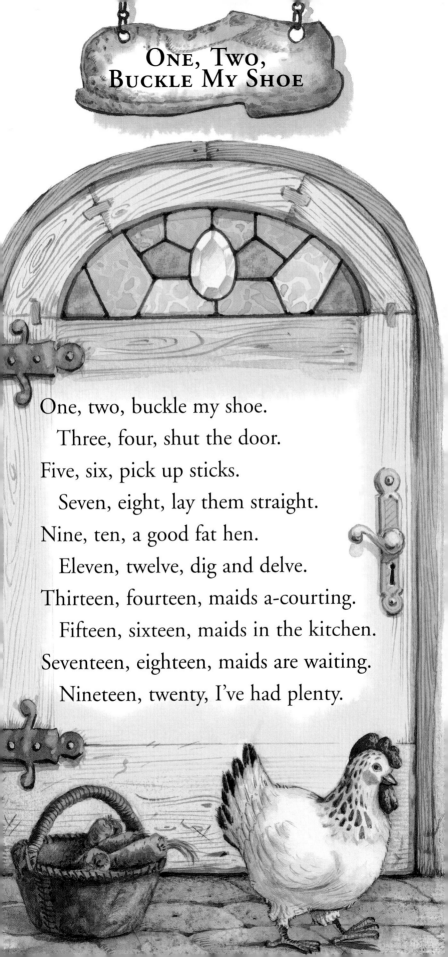

# One, Two, Buckle My Shoe

One, two, buckle my shoe.
  Three, four, shut the door.
Five, six, pick up sticks.
  Seven, eight, lay them straight.
Nine, ten, a good fat hen.
  Eleven, twelve, dig and delve.
Thirteen, fourteen, maids a-courting.
  Fifteen, sixteen, maids in the kitchen.
Seventeen, eighteen, maids are waiting.
  Nineteen, twenty, I've had plenty.

# SIMPLE SIMON

Simple Simon met a pieman
    Going to the fair.
Said Simple Simon to the pieman,
    "Let me taste your ware."

Said the pieman to Simple Simon,
    "Show me first your penny."
Said Simple Simon to the pieman,
    "Indeed, I have not any."

Simple Simon went a-fishing,
    Angling for a whale;
All the water he could find
    Was in his mother's pail.

He went to ride a spotted cow
    That had a little calf;
She threw him down upon the ground,
    Which made the people laugh.

Simple Simon went to see
    If plums grew on a thistle.
He pricked his fingers very much,
    Which made poor Simon whistle.

He went for water with a sieve,
    But soon it all ran through.
And now poor Simple Simon
    Bids you all adieu.

# LITTLE MISS MUFFET

Little Miss Muffet
Sat on a tuffet,
Eating her curds and whey.
Along came a spider,
Who sat down beside her,
And frightened Miss Muffet away.

# Peter, Peter, Pumpkin Eater

Peter, Peter, pumpkin eater,
Had a wife and couldn't keep her.
He put her in a pumpkin shell,
And there he kept her very well.

# ONCE I SAW A LITTLE BIRD

Once I saw a little bird
    Come hop, hop, hop.
So I cried, "Little bird,
    Will you stop, stop, stop?"

I was going to the window
    To say, "How do you do?"
But he shook his little tail,
    And away he flew.

# THREE BLIND MICE

Three blind mice!
    Three blind mice!
See how they run!
    See how they run!
They all ran after the farmer's wife,
Who cut off their tails
    with a carving knife.
Did you ever see
    such a sight in your life
As three blind mice?

# LONDON BRIDGE

London Bridge is falling down,
Falling down, falling down.
London Bridge is falling down,
My fair lady.

Take a key and lock her up,
Lock her up, lock her up.
Take a key and lock her up,
My fair lady.

However will we build it up,
Build it up, build it up?
However will we build it up,
My fair lady?

Build it up with silver and gold,
Silver and gold, silver and gold.
Build it up with silver and gold,
My fair lady.

Gold and silver I have none,
I have none, I have none.
Gold and silver I have none,
My fair lady.

Build it up with needles and pins,
Needles and pins, needles and pins.
Build it up with needles and pins,
My fair lady.

Pins and needles bend and break,
Bend and break, bend and break.
Pins and needles bend and break,
My fair lady.

Build it up with wood and clay,
Wood and clay, wood and clay.
Build it up with wood and clay,
My fair lady.

Wood and clay will wash away,
Wash away, wash away.
Wood and clay will wash away,
My fair lady.

Build it up with stone so strong,
Stone so strong, stone so strong.
Build it up with stone so strong,
My fair lady.

Stone so strong will last so long,
Last so long, last so long.
Stone so strong will last so long,
My fair lady.

# OLD MOTHER HUBBARD

Old Mother Hubbard
   Went to the cupboard
      To fetch her poor dog a bone.
But when she got there
   The cupboard was bare,
      And so the poor dog had none.

She went to the baker's
To buy him some bread,
But when she came back
The poor dog was dead.

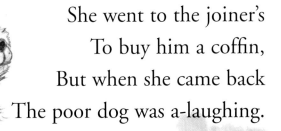

She went to the joiner's
To buy him a coffin,
But when she came back
The poor dog was a-laughing.

She took a clean dish,
To get him some tripe,
But when she came back
He was smoking a pipe.

She went to the tavern
For white wine and red,
But when she came back
The dog stood on his head.

She went to the grocer's
To buy him some fruit,
But when she came back
He was playing the flute.

She went to the hosier's
To buy him some hose,
But when she came back
He was dressed in his clothes.

She went to the tailor's
To buy him a coat,
But when she came back
He was riding a goat.

She went to the barber's
To buy him a wig,
But when she came back
He was dancing a jig.

She went to the cobbler's
To buy him some shoes,
But when she came back
He was reading the news.

The dame made a curtsey,
The dog made a bow;
She said, "Your servant."
The dog said, "Bow wow."

# ONE, TWO, THREE, FOUR, FIVE

One, two, three, four, five!
   Once I caught a fish alive.
Six, seven, eight, nine, ten!
   Then I let it go again.
Why did I let it go?
   Because it bit my finger so.
Which finger did it bite?
   The little finger on the right.

# Jack Sprat

Jack Sprat could eat no fat;
His wife could eat no lean.
And so betwixt the two of them
They licked the platter clean.

# BAA, BAA, BLACK SHEEP

Baa, baa, black sheep,
Have you any wool?
Yes, sir, yes, sir,
Three bags full:

One for my master,
One for my dame,
And one for the little boy
Who lives down the lane.

# HERE WE GO 'ROUND THE MULBERRY BUSH

Here we go 'round the mulberry bush,
The mulberry bush,
The mulberry bush.
Here we go 'round the mulberry bush,
So early in the morning.

This is the way we wash our hands,
Wash our hands,
Wash our hands.
This is the way we wash our hands,
So early in the morning.

This is the way we brush our hair,
Brush our hair,
Brush our hair.
This is the way we brush our hair,
So early in the morning.

This is the way we go to school,
Go to school,
Go to school.
This is the way we go to school,
So early in the morning.

Here we go 'round the mulberry bush,
The mulberry bush,
The mulberry bush.
Here we go 'round the mulberry bush,
So early in the morning.

# To Market, to Market

To market, to market
to buy a fat pig.
Home again, home again, jiggety jig.

To market, to market
to buy a fat hog.
Home again, home again, jiggety jog.

To market, to market
to buy a plum bun.
Home again, home again, market is done.

# PAT-A-CAKE

Pat-a-cake, pat-a-cake, baker's man,
Bake me a cake as fast as you can.
Roll it and pat it and mark it with a "B,"
And put it in the oven for baby and me!

# LITTLE BOY BLUE

Little Boy Blue, come blow your horn.
The sheep are in the meadow,
The cows are in the corn.

Where is the boy
Who looks after the sheep?
He's under the haystack, fast asleep.

Will you wake him?
No, not I,
For if I do, he's sure to cry.

PUSSYCAT,
PUSSYCAT

"Pussycat, pussycat,
        where have you been?"
"I've been to London
        to visit the queen."
"Pussycat, pussycat,
        what did you there?"
"I frightened a little mouse
        under her chair!"

# PEASE PORRIDGE

Pease porridge hot!
Pease porridge cold!
Pease porridge in the pot,
Nine days old.

Some like it hot,
Some like it cold,
Some like it in the pot,
Nine days old!

Hot cross buns!
      Hot cross buns!
One a penny,
      two a penny,
Hot cross buns!
If you have no daughters,
      give them to your sons!

# THE HOUSE THAT JACK BUILT

This is the house
　　that Jack built.

This is the malt
That lay in the house
　　that Jack built.

This is the rat
That ate the malt
That lay in the house
　　that Jack built.

This is the cat
That killed the rat
That ate the malt
That lay in the house
    that Jack built.

This is the dog
That worried the cat
That killed the rat
That ate the malt
That lay in the house
    that Jack built.

This is the cow with
    the crumpled horn
That tossed the dog
That worried the cat
That killed the rat
That ate the malt
That lay in the house
    that Jack built.

This is the maiden all forlorn
That milked the cow
    with the crumpled horn
That tossed the dog
That worried the cat
That killed the rat
That ate the malt
That lay in the house
    that Jack built.

This is the man all tattered and torn
That kissed the maiden all forlorn
That milked the cow
    with the crumpled horn
That tossed the dog
That worried the cat
That killed the rat
That ate the malt
That lay in the house that Jack built.

This is the priest all shaven and shorn
That married the man
    all tattered and torn
That kissed the maiden
    all forlorn
That milked the cow
    with the crumpled horn
That tossed the dog
That worried the cat
That killed the rat
That ate the malt
That lay in the house
    that Jack built.

This is the cock that crowed
    in the morn
That waked the priest
    all shaven and shorn
That married the man
    all tattered and torn

That kissed the maiden all forlorn
That milked the cow
    with the crumpled horn
That tossed the dog
That worried the cat
That killed the rat
That ate the malt
That lay in the house
    that Jack built.

This is the farmer sowing the corn
That kept the cock
    that crowed in the morn
That waked the priest
    all shaven and shorn
That married the man
    all tattered and torn
That kissed the maiden all forlorn
That milked the cow
    with the crumpled horn
That tossed the dog
That worried the cat
That killed the rat
That ate the malt
That lay in the house
    that Jack built.

# OLD KING COLE

Old King Cole was a merry old soul,
And a merry old soul was he.
He called for his pipe,
                   and he called for his bowl,
And he called for his fiddlers three.
Now every fiddler had a fine fiddle,
And a very fine fiddle had he.
Tweedle dum, tweedle dee,
                   went the fiddlers three,
Tweedle dum, tweedle dee, tweedle dee.

# LITTLE BO PEEP

Little Bo Peep has lost her sheep,
And can't tell where to find them.
Leave them alone and they'll come home,
Wagging their tails behind them.

# JACK BE NIMBLE

Jack be nimble,
    Jack be quick,
Jack jump over
    the candlestick.

# PETER PIPER

Peter Piper picked a peck
                 of pickled peppers.
A peck of pickled peppers
                 Peter Piper picked.
If Peter Piper picked
                 a peck of pickled peppers,
Where's the peck of pickled peppers
                 Peter Piper picked?

# There Was a Crooked Man

There was a crooked man,
Who walked a crooked mile.

He found a crooked sixpence,
Against a crooked stile.

He bought a crooked cat,
Which caught a crooked mouse,

And they all lived together
In a crooked little house.

# THREE LITTLE KITTENS

Three little kittens lost their mittens
And they began to cry,
"Oh, mother dear, we sadly fear
Our mittens we have lost!"
"What! Lost your mittens,
        you naughty kittens!
Then you shall have no pie."
*Meow, meow, meow. . . .*
"No, you shall have no pie!"

The three little kittens
        found their mittens
And they began to cry,
"Oh, mother dear, see here, see here,
For we have found our mittens!"
"Put on your mittens, you silly kittens;
Then you shall have some pie."
*Purr, purr, purr. . . .*
"Oh, let us have some pie!"

The three little kittens
        put on their mittens

And soon ate up the pie.
"Oh, mother dear, we greatly fear
Our mittens we have soiled."
"What, soiled your mittens?
        You naughty kittens!"
Then they began to sigh.
*Meow, meow, meow. . . .*
Then they began to sigh.

The three little kittens
        washed their mittens
And hung them up to dry.
"Oh, mother dear, look here, look here,
Our mittens we have washed."
"What, washed your mittens,
        you darling kittens!
But I smell a rat close by!
*Hush! Hush! Hush!*
I smell a rat close by."

# Mary Had a Little Lamb

Mary had a little lamb,
Its fleece was white as snow.
Everywhere that Mary went,
The lamb was sure to go.

It followed her to school one day,
Which was against the rules.
It made the children laugh and play,
To see a lamb at school.

And so the teacher turned him out,
But still he lingered near,
And waited patiently about
Till Mary did appear.

"What makes the lamb love Mary so?"
The eager children cry.
"Oh, Mary loves the lamb, you know,"
The teacher did reply.

# Hickory Dickory Dock

Hickory dickory dock,

    The mouse ran up the clock.

The clock struck one,

    And down he came.

Hickory dickory dock!

# DING, DONG, BELL

Ding, dong, bell, pussy's in the well.
Who put her in?
        Little Johnny Green.
Who pulled her out?
        Little Tommy Stout.
What a naughty boy was that,
To try to drown poor pussy cat,
Who never did him any harm,
And killed the mice in his father's barn.

# THE QUEEN OF HEARTS

The Queen of Hearts,
She made some tarts,
All on a summer's day.

The Knave of Hearts
He stole the tarts,
And took them clean away.

The King of Hearts
Called for the tarts
With a mighty roar.

The Knave of Hearts
Brought back the tarts
And vowed he'd steal no more.

# THERE WAS AN OLD WOMAN

There was an old woman
       Who lived in a shoe.
She had so many children,
       She didn't know what to do.

She gave them some broth
       Without any bread,
Whipped them all soundly,
       And sent them to bed.

# Ring Around the Roses

Ring around the roses,
    A pocketful of posies,
Ashes! Ashes!
    We all fall down!

# RAIN, RAIN, GO AWAY

Rain, rain, go away.
Come again another day.
Little Johnny wants to play.

## THIRTY DAYS HATH SEPTEMBER

Thirty days hath September,
April, June, and November;
February has twenty-eight alone.
All the rest have thirty-one.
Except in leap year. That's the time
When February's days are twenty-nine.

# MONDAY'S CHILD

Monday's child is fair of face.
Tuesday's child is full of grace.
Wednesday's child is full of woe.
Thursday's child has far to go.
Friday's child is loving and giving.
Saturday's child works hard for a living.
But the child that's born
on the Sabbath day.
Is fair and wise and good and gay.

# The Seasons

Spring is showery, flowery, bowery.

Summer: hoppy, croppy, poppy.

Autumn: wheezy, sneezy, freezy.

Winter: slippy, drippy, nippy.

# WEE WILLIE WINKIE

Wee Willie Winkie
    Runs through the town,
Upstairs and downstairs,
    In his nightgown.

Rapping at the window,
    Crying through the lock,
"Are the children all in bed?
    For now it's eight o'clock."

# DIDDLE, DIDDLE, DUMPLING

Diddle, diddle, dumpling,
  my son, John,
Went to bed
  with his trousers on,

One shoe off
  and one shoe on!
Diddle, diddle, dumpling,
  my son, John!

74

# THIS LITTLE PIGGY

This little piggy went to market.
This little piggy stayed home.

This little piggy had roast beef.
This little piggy had none.

And this little piggy cried,
"Wee, wee, wee!"
All the way home.

# Hush-a-Bye, Baby

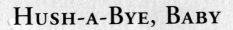

Hush-a-bye, baby, on the tree top.

When the wind blows,
       the cradle will rock.

When the bough breaks,
       the cradle will fall—

Down will come baby,
       cradle and all.